Every Way I Know How

Ten Erotic Stories

Robin Downey

Written by Robin Elizabeth Downey
Some rights reserved
©(i)($)(o)

Cover image by Egon Schiele
Two Women Embracing
Public Domain

ISBN 13: 978-1-928171-13-3 (pbk)
ISBN 13: 978-1-928171-14-0 (ebk)

Vocamus Community Publications
130 Dublin Street, North
Guelph, Ontario, Canada
N1H 4N4

www.vocamus.net

2015

To the father of my children
    – who knows that some of this is true.

Introduction

A book of erotica shouldn't require much introduction, but there are some things I'd like to say before anyone has a chance to complain about them.

First, I sometimes hear that my stories take too long to get to the sex, and it's true that they take longer than most, because my stories aren't actually about sex – they're about people. They certainly do involve sex, of course, but if you're looking for the size of her tits and the length of his cock by the first paragraph and an unlikely simultaneous orgasm by the third, you should probably stick to *Penthouse Letters*.

Second, because I tell stories from the perspective of characters who are female and male, queer and straight, old and young, I'm sometimes accused of presuming to speak for these people, and there's truth to this. Every writer does it. But it's also true that, no matter what characters I write, I can only ever use my own voice. I don't claim to speak for anyone else. I can only speak about what I myself have experienced and observed and sometimes only fantasized. I'm sure that I misrepresent people at times, but that's the nature of writing.

Every Way I Know How

"When we get to the hotel," she said, "I'm going to screw you every way I know how." It was meant more to relieve her boredom than to provoke Richard's libido, but saying it turned her on a little. She visualized them flinging open the door of the room, tossing their baggage on the floor, tearing each other's clothes off as they threw the lock.

"We don't get the room for another five hours, Sylvie," he said, not looking up from his paper. "There's no use getting yourself worked up." He was right, but it didn't make the idea any less attractive.

She sipped her coffee, set it back on the cafe table. Her clothes were wrinkled and dirty from hours on the train. She smelled like body odour and train station. She revised her plans. "Actually," she said, "We're going to shower first. Then I'm going to screw you every way I know how."

"You're not helping anything," he said.

"I'll probably start by sucking your dick," she said. She imagined him stepping from the hotel bathroom, fresh from the shower, ready for the taking.

"Stop it, Sylvie." He set the paper down, adjusted

1

his pants. "You're turning me on, and there's nothing we can do about it."

"I'm sure this place has a bathroom," she said. She was only teasing, but for a moment she wondered what it would be like, sneaking off to the bathroom with him, having him take her in one of the stalls. Too unhygienic for her tastes.

"I don't need to get arrested for public indecency in a strange city," Richard said.

"We're always in a strange city," she replied. "Always." She drained her coffee as she saw the waiter approaching.

He refilled their mugs. "Would you like to order anything?" he asked.

"No thanks," said Richard. "Coffee is fine." It was also about all they could afford, and the waiter looked as if he knew it.

"I'm going to the bathroom," Sylvie said when she was sure the waiter was out of hearing. "Are you coming?" He ignored her, stirred sugar into his coffee by the spoonful.

There was no one in the bathroom when she had finished with the toilet, so she took some time to fix herself up in the mirror. She noticed that the bathroom's outer door had a lock on the inside, imagined Richard walking in, turning the lock, bending her over the counter. He would never do it, but the thought excited her. She went over to the door and locked it herself, just as she imagined he would, then she pulled her skirt up on her thighs and began to stroke herself through her panties.

She was too nervous about being interrupted to keep at it very long, but before unlocking the door she washed her hands again and then, on impulse, pulled off her panties and put them in her purse.

She made her way back to the table, as aroused as she could remember herself ever being. "Hey Richard," she said as she sat.

"Yeah?" He looked up from the paper that he was reading for the third time now.

"I'm not wearing any panties."

"What?"

"You heard me." She leaned forward across the table. "And I've revised my plan again." She tapped the table with a finger. "First, you're going to bend me over the bed and take me hard." She tapped a second finger. "Then we'll have a shower." She tapped a third. "Then I'll suck your cock. And then," she tapped the fourth, "then I'm going to screw you every way I know how."

"Damn it, Sylvie! You're making me crazy here."

"If you're really good," she said, ignoring his complaint, "I might even let you do me in the ass." It was unlikely, but she knew the idea would drive him over the edge. Besides, you never knew. Sometimes she did get that crazy in the heat of things.

He threw the paper onto one of the empty chairs. "I'm going to the bathroom," he said.

"Can I come?"

"No!" He sounded exasperated as he headed toward the back of the cafe.

"Well, no jacking off in there," she called after him, loud enough that people could probably hear her. "That cock is mine today." He ignored her.

She leaned back in her chair and closed her eyes, picturing Richard standing over the toilet, stroking himself at the thought of her. She rubbed her thighs together a little, not enough to draw attention to herself, she hoped, but enough for a little sensation. She thought she could smell her own sex.

She heard Richard sit again and opened her eyes. The waiter was back, but he wasn't offering to refill their coffees. "Will you be ordering something else, or will I be getting your bill?" he asked. He was more tactful than most.

"Just the bill," said Richard. He and Sylvie knew by now when it was time to leave. He put five dollars on the table, barely enough to cover the coffees, but all they had. Sylvie dug the last few coins from her purse by way of a tip.

The waiter nodded at them, probably surprised that they had managed a tip at all. "Have a good day," he said, gathering the money into his belt.

Richard and Sylvie hoisted their bags. Sylvie felt hers catch the hem of her dress, and she wondered how much people saw before she was able to pull it back down.

4

Served her right for not wearing underwear, but she was enjoying the sensation too much to care. All she wanted was a place to fuck – a bed, a couch, even the backseat of a car would do, though she had never much enjoyed that arrangement.

The street was full of office workers at this time of day, coming up to noon, and the sun was bright, hot. She felt like a small point of sex drifting in a sea of passionless business suits. There was nowhere for the two of them to go.

"Maybe the hotel will let us check in early," Richard suggested, but they both knew better.

Sylvie caught sight of something like an alley to their left. She had no idea where it led, but it was better than a street full of suits baking in the heat. She pulled Richard's arm, and he trailed after her. The alley led onto a covered walk, then down a flight of steps into what looked like a storage room, full of empty beer kegs and equipment.

"Where the hell are we?" asked Richard.

"I don't know," Sylvie said, "but it's quiet, and it's cool, and it's free."

He put his bag down on the floor, sat on one of the kegs. "So we'll just sit here until check-in?"

She shrugged. "I'm still not wearing any panties."

His head whipped around in her direction, his eyes looking a little savage. "Don't start that shit again!

Don't even mention sex again until I can do something about it."

There was something in her that wanted to soothe him, but it was small beside the part that just needed to be fucked. She stood, turned her back to him, and leaned over one of the empty kegs. She could tell that its rim would press uncomfortably into her forearms, but she spread her feet apart anyway, tilted her ass up to him, pulled her dress up high enough to expose all of her. "Then do something about it," she said.

The sound he made was almost animal, a groan and a whimper both together. She turned away from him, but heard him fumbling at his belt, dropping his pants, spitting into his hand. She felt his wet fingers stroking desperately at her pussy, moistening her for his cock, and then he was in her, thrusting wildly, his hands gripping her hips, pulling her back against him with every stroke.

She knew it wouldn't take him long like this. His rhythm quickened, and then he stopped altogether, pressing into her, his body rigid, his cock rocking inside her.

He almost collapsed across her body, pressing her arms into the keg in a way that would soon be unbearable. "I can't keep going like this," he said. "I need a place to stop. Even just for a while."

"I know," she said, pushing the two of them to a standing position. She let her skirt fall back into place, felt wetness trickling down her thighs. "I've revised my plan again. We'll go back to the hotel, have a shower,

6

then we'll make some long term decisions."

He nodded. "That sounds good."

"Then," she said, "then I'm going to screw you every way I know how."

Just the One Bedroom

"Sascha?" I said, holding the phone between my ear and my shoulder as I pulled my bag from the taxi. "It's Isabelle."

"Isabelle! How are you? Are you still in Kenora, or have you moved again?"

"I'm actually right in front of your house. I think. 95 Bethany?"

"What? Yeah. That's my place."

The front door of the tiny bungalow swung open, and Sascha leaned out as far as she could without stepping her sock feet in the snow. "Come on in."

I hung up the phone and negotiated the slush along the sidewalk to the door. "You look good," I said, using my mock sexy voice, and she did look good, even better than when I had last seen her, more womanly now, fuller.

She hugged me hard, her hands up between my shoulder blades, pressing our faces together. The smell of her was full of memory – highschool evenings on her couch, watching movies, too afraid to touch her how I wanted.

"How long are you in town?" she asked, drawing me through the door after her.

9

"Maybe for good," I said, a decision that still had to be firmly made, but one that was growing firmer all the time as whatever drive had sent me spinning across the continents gradually wore out its momentum.

"Seriously?" Sascha looked disbelieving, her pale eyebrows making exaggerated arches. "But you can't stay in the same spot for a month at a time." She laughed. "Sometimes you leave a place before you even get there."

She hung my coat and led me into the kitchen. "Sit," she said. "I'll make tea. You talk."

The red of her hair was catching the light of the afternoon sun through the window, so I didn't sit yet, went to hug her again, trailed my fingers through the length of her hair.

"Sit," she said again. "Explain to me how it is that you're finally staying put."

I took one of the wooden chairs at the kitchen table, armless, with padded seat cushions. "There's not much to explain," I said. "I was sitting in Kenora, in my apartment, and just realized that I was tired of it. Always travelling. Always moving. So I sold my car and bought a plane ticket to Toronto. I had the airport taxi take me straight here."

"Where are you staying?" The kettle was now on the stove and the infuser filled with what looked like green tea of some kind.

"Here?" I asked, "Until I find a place?"

Sascha scrunched up her face. "That would be awesome. But all three bedrooms are taken." She put two teacups on the table. "You could maybe use the couch, but my roommates are always up playing video games half the night. I'm not sure how well that would work."

I didn't push her, let her pour the hot water, set the teapot on the table. She sat across from me, her loose blouse clinging to her body, showing the soft roundness of the sports bra that she preferred. It was a practical choice she had insisted when I first asked her about it, years ago now, never suspecting that I would never again be able to see a woman in a sports bra without thinking of her, without desiring her.

"I've got a friend who has a spare room," she said. "I could give her a call?" She said it so sweetly, so innocently, so everything that I needed after all my time away, that I stood and straddled her lap, pulled her head against my chest, kissed the top of her head.

"I'd rather just share your room until we can get an apartment together."

Sascha leaned back, her face full of pleasure. "Yeah. A little two bedroom apartment. Then I wouldn't have to put up with Tommy and Gabriel."

I stroked her hair. She felt wonderful between my thighs, how I had always imagined she would feel, as if she fit me. "Exactly," I said. "We'll get our own place, just like we planned in highschool."

She ducked her head at that, but not in time to cover

11

her look of bitterness. "When you took off to New York on me, you mean. And I had to bail on the apartment we picked."

"I'm sorry," I said, and I was. "I was young, and I wanted to get away from my life, and I was only thinking about myself." She looked up just long enough to meet my eyes, as if checking them for sincerity. "I won't stop apologizing until you forgive me," I told her.

She reached her hands up between my shoulders to give me her peculiar hug, her face pressing my breasts, and I wanted so badly to kiss her. "I already forgive you," she said. "It's just hard to believe that you're really sticking around this time." She released me. "Now sit on your chair and drink your tea," she said. "It's getting cold."

I ordered in Thai food that night, enough for her roommates too, though they didn't bother to sit at the table, only heaped their plates full and headed to the couch and their video game – some first-person shooter indistinguishable from all the others.

Sascha and I moved my few things into her room after supper. I only needed a single drawer in her dresser and a few hangers in her closet. It felt like her life had suddenly enveloped mine, but it was a good feeling. There was a safety to it after so long worrying about what I would do next, where I would go, how I would pay my way.

We spent the evening laying on her bed watching a movie on the little television propped on her dresser –

some sci-fi thing that didn't have much plot but that blew up enough stuff to satisfy some obscure and probably unworthy need in us. We propped our heads on pillows against the wall, drawing the blanket up over our knees. I entwined my arm with hers in a way I had never dared when we were girls. I could feel her body swell and fall with her breathing.

"I'm tired," I said, when it was done. "Jetlag," and I would have laid down right then, but Sascha dragged me out of bed to brush my teeth.

The bathroom was small for two people to brush their teeth together, even smaller when Gabriel came in to pee right there in front of us, showing no apparent embarrassment.

"You're staying the night?" he asked.

"Maybe a few nights," I said.

"I knew it," he said, nudging Sascha with his elbow and sprinkling piss on the toilet seat. "I knew you were a lesbo."

"I'm not a lesbian," she said.

"It explains why you won't screw me."

"There are infinite reasons why I won't screw you." She put her toothbrush back in the cabinet. "In fact, I'd become a lesbian just to avoid screwing you."

He laughed and jiggled the last few drops into the toilet. "How about you, Isabelle?" He tore a piece of toilet paper and wiped the seat. "My bedroom's just down the hall. You can visit any time you like."

"Tempting," I said, "but I'm afraid you'll be sleeping alone tonight."

"Like every night," Tommy called from the other room.

Gabriel laughed with Tommy, seemed not mind his rejection, only washed his hands and went back to his video games.

"He's not always like that," Sascha whispered. "He's just trying to impress you."

"Doing a great job," I said. "But at least he cleans up after himself."

"I've trained them both pretty well." She smirked. "Now get out. I have to pee."

I wandered down to the bedroom, changed into the long t-shirt that served as my pyjamas, laid down on the bed with the covers pulled back. My belly was full of anticipation, with the unexpected possibility, long imagined, soon to be realized, that I would share a bed with her. My sex moistened at the thought of it, an ache at my centre.

Sascha entered the room and closed the door behind her. Her eyes found mine as she undid the top buttons of her blouse. She turned away from me. "Changing might be a bit weird," she said, and she pulled the shirt over her head, tossing it into the closet laundry basket.

"There's nothing to be weird about," I said. "I think you look beautiful," but she hesitated to remove her bra, slipped down her peasant skirt instead. She stood there in her underclothes – plain white sports bra and plain

14

pink panties – hanging her skirt in the closet, and I couldn't resist her ant longer.

She heard me getting up from the bed and turned, her hands coming up to cover her breasts. I wrapped my arms around her, laying my face on her shoulder, kissing the shape of her collarbone.

"You're different than when you left," she said, but it was more observation than accusation.

"Not really," I told her. "I'm just not as scared."

The idea seemed to take her by surprise, distract her from our embrace. "How do you not be scared?"

"New York," I said, "Tampa Bay, the Azores, Brussels, Seattle, Vancouver, Kenora, and now home."

"I guess," she said, and she was quiet a moment. "But how do I know you'll stay this time?"

I pulled the strap of her bra down her shoulder, kissed the top of her breast. "New York," I said. I turned and pulled down the other strap. "Tampa Bay." I tugged the tight fabric away to release her breasts, their small, light nipples. "The Azores." I kissed one nipple to hardness. "Brussels." I kissed the other, then suckled it more deeply. "Seattle." I kissed up her chest and her neck. "Vancouver." I kissed along her chin and jaw. "Kenora." I put my mouth on hers, let my tongue run along her lips, felt her respond. "And now home."

Her breath was heavy and ragged. I slipped my hands into the waist of her panties, knelt as I drew them down her thighs and calves, kissed at her pussy as she stepped out of them. I pulled my own shirt over my head as I rose, saw her removing her bra, and we stood face to face, our hands entwined, our bodies lightly brushing at hip and breast.

I led her to the bed and pulled the covers over us, beginning with her lips now and moving down her body, kissing along her curves and swells, tasting her skin. She wrapped me loosely with her arms, spread her legs around me, made hardly a sound as I traced her body with my mouth. Only the depth of her breathing betrayed her pleasure.

She gasped once when my mouth found her pussy, when I spread her with my tongue, and then she was quiet once more, pressing the wetness of her sex against the wetness of my mouth. I filled myself with the taste of her, with the taste of sex and sweat and desire, rolling her over on top of me, letting her thrust on my tongue until I felt her body quieten. Then I held her to me, my face against her belly, my own ache still unsated but somehow tranquil.

"We should go looking for apartments tomorrow," she said.

"Yeah," I told her. "A little two bedroom place just for us."

"Well," she said, "just the one bedroom might be enough."

A Decent Exhibit

"It's a decent exhibit," Jacob said. "Not really my thing, but decent."

"I really like her stuff," said Rowland, "especially the series of houses at night."

"Too representational for me."

Rowland shrugged.

"And she's so damn skinny," Jacob said. "Got to be anorexic or something." They both looked to where Lena was showing a group of people one of her paintings. She was wearing a designer sweater that left one shoulder bare down to the middle of her arm. It was loose, but it clung to her, shaping itself to her small, clearly braless breasts.

"She's not that skinny," said Rowland. "And she eats lots, probably more than I do."

"I didn't know you guys were such close friends."

"Not friends exactly. We were in the same program. Only she was good, and I wasn't. That's why she has the show, and I'm just hosting it."

Jacob jingled the icecube in his almost empty glass of scotch. "So you've never slept with her."

"Of course not."

He bit a chunk from the icecube and let the rest of it fall back into his glass. "Her face always tempts me to take a shot." He wrinkled up his face. "But then I see those tiny tits and that skinny ass, and I just can't do it."

Rowland shook his head. "I'm sure she appreciates your restraint."

"Plus, she always acts like she's better than me."

"She is better than you."

"I meant as an artist, not as a person."

"I meant as both."

Jacob smirked, then frowned. "Oh, shit. She's coming over." He patted Rowland's arm. " I'll leave you two alone. I've got better things to do than put up with her ego." He drifted toward the bar, raising his empty glass to attract the bartender's attention."

"Rowland," said Lena, and she placed her hand on his elbow, leaned in to kiss the air by his cheek. "Thanks so much for this. You've put on a great event." Her voice was as formal as her kiss.

"Your work deserves it," Rowland said. "We even sold some things."

"I know." A smile of bemusement broke her carefully maintained detachment. "Alexis Havelid bought one of the evening cityscapes."

"I may have encouraged her in that direction."

"Thanks. I'm just relieved that things went well." She leaned her head back as if stretching her neck. "Now I have to survive the come-down."

"The come-down?"

"Yeah, you know, when you get all geared up for something, and then it's over, and you finally have time to crash. It can be intense for me. I get pretty depressed."

"I see."

"My Mom used to hold me together after these things, but North Bay is a long way from Toronto, and the phone just doesn't cut it."

"Well, I'm not your mom, but you can give me a shout if you want."

She smiled for a moment, quickly resumed her professional demeanour. The two of them stood silently in the midst of the swirling guests and the low chatter, looking into their drinks, though his was long empty and hers looked like it hadn't been touched all night.

"I think what I want," she said, looking up, "is for you to have sex with me."

"Excuse me?"

"It won't fix anything," she said, "but maybe it'll put off my come-down until tomorrow." There was a pleading in her voice, and Rowland was uncertain how to answer her.

"Are you sure that's a good reason to sleep with me?" he asked at last.

19

"I don't really care," she said. "I've known you for-ever, and you're a good guy, and you're unattached, and I just want you to have sex with me." She was quiet for a moment, and so was he. "I mean, if you want."

Rowland looked away for a moment, as if he was searching for someone else to give an opinion. "I won't be done until really late," he said, still looking away from her, "but I could come by your place when I'm done cleaning up."

"We can do that too," she said, "but I want it now."

"Now?"

"Yeah. There's a couch in your office. Let's do it now."

There was a long pause between them, and then Row-land turned back to her decisively, as if he had settled the question in his own mind. He pulled his office key from his pocket and handed it to her. "I'll tell Sarah that I'm going to take care of some things. I'll meet you in in ten minutes."

She took the key wordlessly, palmed it, like a dealer or a spy. Rowland watched her as she walked to the back doors toward his office. He didn't move until she had disappeared, then he turned to the island that served as a sales centre at the front of the gallery space. Sarah was sitting there, chatting up some potential buyers.

"...here until the 28th," she was saying. "Come back any time. I can help you make a choice that would suit your needs."

"I think we will," said the older gentleman, though he directed this more to the younger woman beside him than to Sarah, and his tone implied that he wasn't likely to do anything of the sort.

"Excuse me, Sarah," Rowland said. "I've just had a call about the Dundas show next week, and I need to take care of it. I'll be back in fifteen."

Sarah waved him away, and he turned toward his office as the young woman at the desk pressed her older companion to book an appointment. Rowland's pace was noticeably erratic, first hurrying, then slowing, then hurrying again. When he passed through the back exit, he no longer made an attempt to hide his haste, jogging to the door of his office.

He opened it to find Lena standing exactly in the centre of his circular office carpet, one heeled foot in front of the other, hands on hips, shoulders slung provocatively, poised, as if she was a manikin or a sculpture. He closed the door behind him, locked it. She pulled her sweater over her head in a single motion, revealing small, jutting breasts, aggressive breasts, her nipples already erect.

He made no attempt to touch her, only began removing his own clothes, fumbling at his tie and collar, prying his shoes off with his feet, awkward in his hurry.

She turned her back to him and slipped the pants off her slim hips, her pants and panties both at once, and she half-knelt on his office couch, her hands resting on its back, her face turned to watch him as he struggled with

21

his clothing.

At last he was naked also, his erection seeming to lead him across the room to kneel on the floor behind her. He took her slim buttocks in his hands, her too delicate body, and he searched out her vagina with his tongue, pressing his face urgently into her. She made no sound, just circled her ass against him, wriggling to his touch, as if willing him to go deeper, to stay longer, but it was not a request he could grant. When he felt her opening to him, he stood, entered her with all at once. Her breath came sharply.

He placed his hands on her ass, thrusting rhythmically, pulling her body against him, but she soon moved of her own accord, no longer needing his leading, so he slid his hands up her thin belly, engulfed her tits with his hands. She made a whimpering sound and began grinding against him, so he did it again, brought his hands down to her belly and up to seize her breasts, and then again, pressing her nipples with his palms.

She reached one hand up between her thighs, began to touch herself as he stroked her breasts with his hands and her pussy with his cock. She circled his shaft with her fingers when he pulled out of her, rubbed herself vigorously when he pressed into her again.

"I'm coming," she said, though only moments could have passed since she had been standing on his carpet. She pressed her face into the top of the couch and groaned.

He straightened himself again, seized her ass in his

hands, thrust urgently into her until his own orgasm shuddered through him. He moved himself gently in her a few times, then pulled away and collapsed onto the couch, half-closed his eyes.

Lena cleaned herself with her panties and tossed them onto his desk. Then she slipped her pants and sweater on, once again detached and professional. "I'll see you out there in a few minutes," she said. She put his office key down beside her panties, put another key beside it. "Here's my apartment key. I'll expect you sometime tonight."

"Yes," he said, "sometime tonight," and she left him, naked and sprawled on his office couch.

We're Gonna Dance

Helen watched Jamie park along the curb. It was the closest spot to Steve's house but still three hundred yards away. The party was still obvious though, even from so far, even in the dark. It was lit up with strands of Christmas lights, incongruous in the August heat, and the music from the backyard was loud enough to penetrate the windows of their car all that way down the street.

Jamie laid his head on the steering wheel.

"It won't be so bad," Helen told him.

"Yeah," he said, "it will be."

"We only get to see some of these people once a year."

"Once a year too often."

"Come on. Just have some fun." She opened the car door. "Have a drink. Dance with me."

He reached into the back seat for the twelve pack of craft beer. "I'm with you on the drinking bit," he said. "But I'll leave the dancing to you."

She took his hand as the sidewalk led them to the side gate of Steve's yard, awash in patio light and music loud enough to prevent useful conversation. There were already forty or fifty people dancing, and the bass trembled through Helen's body. She tried to pull Jamie along with her into the midst of the dancers, but he twisted away, heading down the slope of the lawn toward a row of kitchen chairs that had been set under the trees.

"Come on, Jamie," she called, not because it would change his mind but because she knew it would irritate him. "Just one dance."

"Nope," he said, turning to walk backwards as he spoke, "You dance. I'll drink."

She turned into the swirl of bodies, almost colliding with a guy she vaguely recognized from highschool, no, from somewhere else.

"Dance?" he asked.

"Sure," she said, and she had the sudden desire to let herself go, to let dancing be what it could be for her, the next thing to sex, in some ways almost better. She slipped her arm around the guy's waist, pulled herself against him, his thigh between her legs.

He pulled away a little. "I'm here with someone," he said.

"So am I." She turned him a little to the left, where Jamie could see her, ground herself against the leg between her thighs, sliding up and down the guy's body.

She looked to where Jamie was sitting. He met her eyes and raised his beer to her in a toast.

She slid her hand up behind her partner's neck, tried to pull him down to kiss her, but he pushed away. "I just wanna dance," he said.

26

"That's how I dance."

"Only if you want my girlfriend to kill you." He retreated through the press of the dance floor.

Helen scanned the faces around her, but there weren't many unattached, none that she recognized. She circled the edge of the crowd toward the DJ booth, almost fell into Tara before recognizing her.

"Tara, I love your hair cut," she said, which was mostly true. The cropped hair looked good on her, carefully sculpted, but Helen had always loved her with long hair, loved how the curls had swayed when Tara was on top of her, hanging like a tent around their faces.

"I'm still getting used to it," Tara said. She took Helen in a loose hug, nothing more than friendly, though she held it far longer than a friend would. "You're still too skinny," she said. "I could pick you up and carry you off."

"I've got pepper spray," Helen said, and she felt Tara's silent laugh.

"Dance with me," said Tara, pulling Helen into the crowd with a kind of slow step, though the music was a club tune, all speed and synthetic drums and repetitious vocals.

Helen slid her arms down to Tara's waist, taking in the voluptuousness of her body. She knew the fullness of it, had many times lost herself in the round thighs and in the huge breasts that were now pressing against her more modest ones. Why had she ever let this go? She

27

put one hand into the back pocket of Tara's jeans and brought the other one up on her hip, slid one of Tara's soft thighs between her own, felt the roughness of denim on the flesh beneath her skirt.

"You're turning me on," Tara said. Her breath was loud in Helen's ear, warm on her neck.

"Should I stop?"

"Hell no."

Helen pressed herself against the other woman in time to the music, gradually drawing the two of them toward the opposite edge of the floor, to where Jamie would be watching. She couldn't see over Tara's shoulder, so she angled their bodies until she could meet Jamie's eyes.

Tara had begun kissing Helen's neck, nuzzling, kissing, nuzzling again. Helen put both her hands on Tara's ass and rocked against her more firmly, no longer even pretending to dance. She wondered if they were attracting attention, but she didn't really care.

Jamie was still sitting in his chair, had just finished a beer, probably his second by now, had put it back into the case, was opening another. He met her eyes and smiled, shook his head in mock dismay.

Tara seemed to sense Helen's distraction, looked over to where Jamie was sitting. He waved.

"Shit," said Tara.

"What?"

"I thought you were here on your own."

"He's my boy," Helen said. "But you could be my girl." She leaned in and kissed the dark skin of Tara's throat. "Like before."

Tara had pulled away a little, still holding Helen's waist, but loosely now, a more tentative intimacy. "God, I want to," she said, then made anguished sound in her throat. "Hell. You know I can't. It would end up like last time. Me jealous. You angry."

"You'd be my only girl. You were always my only girl."

"It's not enough." She looked to where Jamie was sipping his beer. "I can't do what he does. Just sit there and watch you with someone else."

"So I can't take you home with me?"

Tara shook her head, more amused than rueful, then nodded in Jamie's direction. "No, you should take him home with you." She kissed Helen quickly four or five times on the forehead.

"But he won't dance."

"Maybe not, but he's a boy who lets you have your girl." He brushed hair back from Helen's face. "Not everyone could." She kissed Helen once more, full on the lips this time. "I know I couldn't."

"Why are you always right?" Helen asked. "You damned, practical woman." They stepped away from each other, still holding hands by the fingers. "Now, if only you knew how to get a man to dance."

29

Tara laughed. "I'm not really the one to ask about men," she said.

Their fingers parted. Helen watched Tara drift away through the crowd. Her body was on edge with desire. Every bit of her seemed primed to screw – no, first to dance, then to screw. She bit her lip and walked down the grassy slope to where Jamie was sitting.

"Done so soon?" he said. He raised his bottle. "I'm only four beers in."

She had begun moving to the music before she even got to him, undulating her hips, running her hands over her body, using every move she had ever watched in the stripper scenes of bad cop flicks.

He laughed. "Have you been drinking, miss?" he asked. "You're supposed to be the designated driver."

She straddled him, not sitting on his lap exactly, but working herself up and down his body, thrusting her breasts in his face. He put his free hand up on her hip, but she slapped it away. "No touching," she said.

She settled herself on his lap now, her bare thighs against his cords, her ass pressing against where his cock lay hidden. She wriggled herself there, ran her hands up her body, cupped her breasts for him.

He groaned.

"So you do like dancing?" she asked, and she undid a button on her shirt, enough to show what little cleavage she had.

He didn't answer, only leaned toward her chest.

She pulled back, shimmying her shoulders, teasing him. "I asked you a question," she said. "Do you like my dancing?"

"Yes, I like your dancing," he said, his voice thick.

She leaned forward and let him nuzzle her breasts, his lips pulling at the flesh as deeply as her bra would allow. "Was that so hard?" she asked, then stood and looked down at him.

He had lost his beer at some point, both his arms dangling at his sides, his face hot with lust.

"Do you want me to dance some more?"

He nodded.

"I need words, mister."

"Yes," he said. "I want to see you dance."

She turned and lowered her ass into his lap again, backwards now, grinding herself against his cock. "Good, she said. "Then do what I tell you." She bounced her ass on him a few times. "Promise me."

He tried to put his hands on her thighs, but she pushed them away again, raised herself from his lap just enough to prevent his pleasure. "Promise."

"I promise," he said.

"That's a good boy." She sat again. "Now undo your pants."

"What?"

"You promised."

"But I..."

"Just do it!"

She felt him fumble at his belt and his button and his zipper.

"Now get your cock out."

"No way!" he whispered, his voice hoarse. "I'm not taking my dick out in front of the whole party."

"Under my skirt," she said. "Get your cock out under my skirt."

"What the fuck's gotten into you?" he asked.

"You wouldn't dance with me. So now I'm dancing with you. That's what the fuck's gotten into me. Now do it." She raised herself enough to flip her skirt up over him. He slipped his hand between their bodies, unzipping, pulling at his boxers, and then she felt his cock between her thighs. She squeezed her thighs around him, undulating on him, letting the music drive her.

"Shit," he said. "You're going to make me come."

She open her thighs, released his cock. "Not yet. Put it in me."

He didn't argue this time, just pulled at her panties, loosening them enough to put his cock inside them. He fumbled with himself, tried to enter her, but couldn't get the angle right. She reached under skirt and placed him at her pussy, leaned back onto him, letting him fill her.

"Hold it as long as you can," she told him. "Cause now we're gonna dance."

She worked herself on his body, twisting and circling and gyrating. He put his hands on her hips, pulling her down against him as he thrust into her. She let her head roll back, noticed that people had begun to stop and look at them, but it only seemed to give more license to her body. She rocked faster onto him, lapping up the pleasure until she felt him spasm.

She slowed her hips to a liesurely roll. "Better get yourself back in your pants," she said. "I'm taking you home with me."

She stood, let her skirt fall back around her, left him arranging himself as she sauntered through the crowd toward their car.

Temporary Accommodations

"Shit!" Gordon said. Alexa saw him stumble back, throw his arm above his head, the bottle sloshing whiskey all down his arm and shoulder. He gave a thick laugh. "I totally didn't see that branch." He was drunk enough at ten o'clock that the evening might as well be over. He'd pass out soon, then she'd have to drag him into the tent, spend the rest of the night listening to his booze-induced snore.

They reached the campsite, and Gord began rummaging through the food pack. "I can't find the cups," he announced after a moment. He picked up the bottle again. "I guess we'll just have to do it the old fashioned way." His words were deeply slurred even before he took a long pull from the bottle. He extended it in no particular direction, as if to the whole of the universe. "Anybody?"

"No thanks. I should sober up," said Dave. "We have to get back to the city yet tonight."

"That's not the man I knew," said Gord. He gestured with the bottle, almost spilling it again.

"The man you knew," Dave said, "didn't have a wife

35

who would kill him for getting a DUI."

"You could stay the night." There was a note of surprised self-congratulation in Gord's voice, as if he had just solved a grave difficulty, world hunger perhaps, or faster than light travel. "There's space in our tent." He swung the hand with the bottle toward the tent that Alexa had brought for the two of them. "It can fit like a hundred people." He laughed at this and said it again. "A hundred people."

"Well nobody's staying in our tent," Lisa said. She was leaning against George on the picnic table. She reached over with her free hand to cup his groin. "I didn't prance around the beach in a bikini all day not to get laid tonight."

Which had been Alexa's plan too, as a matter of fact. Not that she had a bikini to prance in. She wasn't really the bikini type, not really the prancing type either, but she had still planned on getting laid tonight, unlikely now that Gordon was sloshing drunk. Even less likely if two other guys hung around to get drunk as well and crash in her tent.

"I was hoping for a little action myself," she said. She tried to sound joking.

"Come on, Lexy," Gord said. His mouth was slack, his face blankly belligerent. "Let's show some hos-pit-ality." He could hardly pronounce this last word, had to break it into syllables.

"This was supposed to be our time away, Gord," she

said. "No kids. Just the two of us." She made no effort now to hide her dissatisfaction.

"We can screw any time, baby." He took a few steps toward Dave and Winston, his arms open. "How often do we bump into old friends?"

"We don't even have extra sleeping bags."

"We've got a beach blanket," Lisa said, "and so do you."

"No, no," said Winston, "we don't want to intrude." His thin face was sharply shadowed under the brim of his Tilley hat.

"The hell we don't," said Dave. "I'll take any excuse not to go home tonight." He grabbed the bottle from Gord and took a swig. He wiped his lips on his sleeve and handed the bottle back. "I'll get a fire going."

"That's my boy!" Gord crowed.

"Gord. Please," Alexa said.

"Stop your whining, Lexy." Gord started shuffling over to the fire pit. "If you're really that horny, you can do me anyway. Have yourself an audience."

"You're a real asshole sometimes, Gord," Alexa said, something she had thought far too often lately. "Fine. Go ahead and get yourself shit-faced. I'm going to bed."

She unzipped the tent and then zipped it behind her with more savagery than it required, turned on the dome light. She pulled her shirt over head and went rummaging in the dufflebag for her pajamas.

There was a scratching at the door of the tent.

"Hello." It was Winston's voice. "Can I come in? Just want to get this blanket laid out while you've still got the light on."

She was just in her bra, and her pajamas were proving elusive, but she wasn't showing much more than her bathing suit had shown that afternoon. "Come on in."

The door zipped, and there was the sound of someone ducking through the flap.

"Sorry," Winston said, when he saw her. "I thought you said come in."

The pajamas were rolled into the side pouch, though she didn't remember putting them there. She turned to where he was half-crouching beneath the low dome of the tent, Lisa's beach blanket hugged in his hands. "I did," she said. "Put your stuff wherever you like."

"Sure," he said, but he just stood there trying not to look at her.

His discomfort flattered her, though she wasn't sure why, and modesty didn't seem like something Gord deserved from her at the moment. She kept her eyes on Winston's face as she reached behind her and unclasped her bra, letting her breasts find their natural shape, different now that three children had nursed them, but still attractive enough to elicit Gord's admiration after thirteen years of marriage.

Winston ducked aside, busied himself with arranging his blanket along the far side of the tent, straightening it unnecessarily, taking far longer than he needed.

38

Alexa took her time too, bent to tuck her shirt and bra into her bag before standing again, her hair brushing static from the ceiling of the tent. She had just begun wiggling out of her jeans when he looked up again, and the sight of her seemed to freeze him half-kneeling on his blanket. Her breasts swung toward his face as she bent to pull the jeans over her calves.

"I should get back to the guys," he said, and he stood, but the low ceiling forced him to bend toward her, and their faces were close as lovers.

She turned to kick her jeans into the open bag, blocking the door with her body. He retreated into the back of the tent, his tall, slender body still hunched, his face turned to avoid the brightness of the dome light and the sight of her body.

"Could you arrange the other blanket for Dave?" she asked. Her question drew his eyes to her involuntarily in time to see her panties slide down her thighs.

He looked resolutely at her face, never once glancing down her naked body. "Where should I put it?"

She gestured to the far side of the tent, as far as possible from where Winston had arranged his own blanket, and he turned to obey, clearly relieved to have the distraction.

He was even longer about it this time, and she took pity on him, dressing herself while his back was turned, so that only a few buttons remained to be fastened by the time he met her eyes again.

39

"Thanks, Winston," she said.

"No problem." He paused. "Winston's actually my last name. My first name's Jeffrey."

"Sure," she said, and she knelt to arrange her own mattress and sleeping bag, sliding them a good distance away from Gord's place, closer to where Winston had laid his blanket.

"I guess I'll get back to the fire," he said again.

She laid herself down and pulled the sleeping bag around her. "Can you turn out the light first?"

He didn't reply, but did as she asked, leaving her in the darkness as he exited the tent and zipped it behind him.

Alone and in the dark, the memory of what she had just done washed arousal through her body. Winston – or Jeffery, she guessed – was a little thin for her taste, but she couldn't help imagining how differently the situation might have ended had he been more forward, if he had taken her nakedness as an invitation. A shudder of desire ran through her, and she trailed her fingers down between her thighs.

She could hear the night noises of crickets and creaking trees, the crackling of the fire, the rise and fall of drunken conversation outside. Gord was telling the story of how his old timers hockey team had been robbed of the championship by a terrible call, a story that had became more embellished with each telling since the spring.

40

She shut out the conversation, tried to sleep, but then there was the sound of Lisa and George going to their tent, just a few feet away, George tripping on one of the tie ropes, the two of them giggling to each other as they closed the tent.

"Where did you put the flashlight?" one of them whispered, the owner of the voice hard to distinguish at such low volume.

"I don't need a light to screw you," the other whispered back.

"I thought you wanted to see me in my bikini," said a voice that must have belonged to Lisa.

"Mmmm. That's right. Let's find the light."

There was a giggle. "You're ridiculous."

"Ridiculously horny. Now find the light."

A light abruptly brightened the side of Alexa's tent.

"Not in my eyes," George said aloud, then back to a whisper. "You've blinded me. I'll have to do everything by feel."

It was Lisa who yelped this time. "Watch where you put your cold hands," she said.

"Hey," Dave yelled from the fire pit. "Keep it down in there. People are trying not to have sex out here."

Gord's laughter came choked, as if he had been in mid-swig.

"That's just jealousy talking," George called back. He was not Alexa's idea of the perfect man, but he was mostly sweet, and he knew when to do what he was told, and he had hung with Lisa even through years of stressful infertility – a step up from Gord anyway.

The tent next door had become quiet except for the rustling sound of clothes being changed and bedding being arranged. Alexa had once more settled herself for sleep when the whispering began again.

"Okay, open your eyes," someone said.

"Oh God, that's hot," George whispered back. "Turn around and show me your ass." A pause. "Shit. I just want to eat that."

A giggle. "Oh, you'll eat it all right."

The light flicked off. "Hands and knees," George whispered, and then a few moments later there was a long, low groan.

"Aren't you going to take them off?"

"No. "I'm going to eat you right through them."

Lisa gave a giggle from her throat. "You really are ridiculous."

Several minutes passed, maybe many. It was hard for Alexa to tell in the dark. The talk at the fire pit had quieted. Even the forest had hushed. The only sound was the sound of George's mouth on Lisa's flesh, their low, entangled, intermittent moans.

Alexa pictured them, Lisa crouched on her forearms, her bikini-covered bottom lifted for George's mouth, his tongue teasing her through the fabric.

Her hand slid to her own sex. She could imagine the taste of Lisa on her tongue, the woman's firm flesh beneath her hands. She had watched Lisa at the beach all afternoon, imagined reaching across the short space of sand between their towels to caress her tanned legs. Now those legs would be spread for George's tongue. She stroked herself at the thought.

"Cock please, George," came Lisa's whisper. "No. Leave them on. Just pull them to the side. Yeah, like that."

Alexa heard him moving in the bedding, then heard Lisa groan, not a whisper, but a full-throated groan. There was a few seconds of quiet, and then the rhythmic sound of his cock in her and their synchronized breathing became the only sound in the nights.

Alexa stroked herself fiercely. She imagined alternately that she was the one bent beneath George's cock or the one between Lisa's thighs, their pussies pressing against each other.

"Shit," George whispered at last. "I'm coming."

"Wait," Lisa whispered. "Just a few...oooh yes. Me too. Me too."

Alexa's own orgasm wouldn't come, though her fingers were desperate. She felt it recede ever further as she heard the lovers disentangle, clean themselves up for bed. Their voices were too low now to make out the words, just murmurs.

Her own sex ached, but she had never been much good at getting herself off. She rolled onto her belly, cupped her sex and tried to grind herself to orgasm, but she knew it was wasted effort.

The fire hissed outside, and she realized that the guys were pissing on it, getting ready for bed. Their footsteps approached the tent, and then the zipper was pulled open.

"This way, Gordo," said the first figure through the door, Dave by his voice.

"I can do it," Gord said. "I'm not that drunk."

"You almost went to the wrong tent."

Gord laughed loudly. "That would've been a good show."

"Shhh," said Winston from outside. "You'll wake Alexa."

"Shit," said Gord. "Old Lexy sleeps like a stone. I can practically screw her and she'll sleep straight through it."

It was Dave who laughed now. "That I believe," he said.

Alexa felt Gord fall onto his sleeping bag, a heavy inanimate sound, then his hand pinched her ass, crept up to grab at her breasts. She pretended sleep.

"See?" he said. "Like a stone. You wanna try."

"I'm not that stupid," said Dave.

The three of them were all in the tent now, the smell of woodsmoke and whiskey heavy in the closeness of the tent. Gord hadn't bothered to get under his blankets at all, hadn't even bothered to take his shoes off, but

44

the other two removed their footwear and tried to cover themselves as best they could with the beach blankets.

It was only a few minutes until Gord was snoring deeply beside her, and soon after she thought she could hear Dave breathing deeply too, but Winston was still clearly awake, turning frequently, trying to make himself comfortable on the hard ground.

Alexa's need had receded a little, but not enough to let her sleep. She watched Winston in the darkness, wondering whether he was thinking of her.

He turned again, and his eyes opened, catching hers.

"Hey," she said. "Are you comfortable?"

He shrugged. "Not really. The ground's hard, and it's freezing."

She lifted the edge of her sleeping bag, though she hadn't planned it. "Come on in," she said. "There's room on the mattress for two, and it's warm in here."

"I don't think that's a good idea," he said. His eyes flicked past her to Gord's sleeping bulk.

"Don't worry about Gord. He won't wake up until at least noon tomorrow."

"That's not really..."

Alexa reached out and took his arm, pulled him toward her. He didn't resist, but he turned his back to her as she arranged the sleeping bag over him, curling his body away from her.

She pressed herself against his back, her desire fully awakened once more, and she slid her hand down the front of him. He didn't move, not once, even as she undid the button on his jeans, pulled open the zipper, worked the denim low enough to take his penis out the top of his boxers. He was hard in her hand, clearly aroused, but his body was unmoving against hers. "I'm gonna stroke your cock good," she whispered in his ear.

He said nothing.

"Why don't you slide you hand back here and give me some stroking too?"

He did move then, reached back as he was told, but woodenly, as if moved against his will. He placed his hand on her ass, cupped it, began to caress it a little.

"You'll need to do better than that," she said. She was stroking his cock seriously now, the way she knew men liked, but she stopped and reached to the hand on her ass, directed it down her pants and further, so that his fingers trailed between her thighs almost against her sex. "That's where I need it, Winston. Right there."

"It's Jeffery," he said, as she returned her hand to his cock, and there was a strange quality to his voice, as if the question of his name had something to do with the way his hand still rested unresponsive on her flesh.

"Okay then," she said. "Jeffrey, I want you to touch me. I want your hands on my ass, Jeffrey, and your fingers in my pussy."

He groaned a little and pulled at her bottom, the first real movement he had made of his own volition.

46

"That's right, Jeffery," she said. "Now fuck me with your fingers, Jeffery. Right here beside my husband."

He half turned against her and pulled her thigh up onto him, then slid his hand down to cup her. He stroked a little, found her wetness, slid a finger into her.

She pressed herself back against his hand, almost too distracted to stroke him in return. She felt a second finger in her, then a third, pulling her open, but his reach wasn't long enough him to enter her deeply. He only added to her desire, did nothing to satisfy it.

Her pants had been pulled halfway down her thighs by now. She took her hand from his cock and pushed the pajama bottoms off all together. The movement pulled his fingers away, and their absence was an ache.

She pulled him onto his back and straddled him, placed his cock against her pussy, settled slowly onto it, let it fill her where her need was. Jeffery lay motionless beneath her, a kind of uncertainty in his face. He raised his hands and began unbuttoning her shirt, until her breasts were bare, but his eyes still seemed to be asking something of her, permission maybe, she didn't know.

"You can fuck me, Jeffery," she said. "I want you to fuck me."

For a moment he only looked at her. "Not Winston," he said, "Jeffery," and then a change came across his face, though she wasn't sure what it meant. He drew her down to him, took a nipple in his mouth, began to fuck her gently.

47

Streaks of Dirt

"You're actually starting to get a tan," she said.

Leo glanced at her, his thin arms straining with their load of flagstone. His eyes seemed to be checking whether she was mocking him. "I've been working in the sun for three weeks now," he said. He set the flagstones down beside the expanse of levelled screenings that was gradually becoming a patio. "It had to happen eventually."

Wendy went to put the shovels and rakes back in the shed, the newly constructed shed, made of rough cedar planks, Leo's previous project. She thought she could feel him watching her.

"Can I borrow your shower again tonight?" he asked. She heard him drink from his water bottle.

"Sure," she said. "Where do you guys go on Friday nights anyway?"

"Just to the bar."

"At 5:30?"

"Well, we grab dinner first, hang-out at somebody's place, have a few drinks before we go." He went back through the gate to the truck, returned with another load.

"So there's no time to go home and shower then?" she asked.

"I could, I guess." His was voice straining with his arms, "But it's half an hour out to my place and then half an hour back. It just saves me time to shower here."

"I see."

He set the stones atop the pile. "You said you didn't mind."

"I don't."

He stretched his back. He was pretty enough in his way, she thought, but too slight a build for this sort of labour. He wouldn't bulk up much either, not if he was like his father. They were both purpose-made for office jobs, the kind of men who looked good in a suit but were out of place in a t-shirt and shorts.

"Is that the last of it?" she asked.

"One more load." He started toward the truck but stopped, his face turning to the ground somewhere near her feet, but his eyes flicking up to catch hers. "Um, Wendy," he said, and he paused, not as if he was thinking what to say, but as if he was summoning the courage to say something that he had long left unsaid, trying to make it seem nonchalant. "You want to join me in the shower today?"

She had just taken the wheelbarrow by the handles, about to put it in the shed also, but his request stopped her, left her trying to figure exactly how to take his request, exactly how to tell him no. "What do you want with an old woman like me in your shower?" she asked, trying to sound playful, hoping that he would pick up her ruse and laugh the situation off, pretend that he had been asking in fun.

He jerked his head away, looked at the pile of stone he had been building for the past hour. "You're not that old," he said.

"I'm thirty-eight," she said. "And what are you? Twenty? I'm almost twice your age."

He looked directly at her. "I don't care."

"Your parents probably will," she said, which was true. Her colleague from work and his wife were as protective of Leo as they were easy going in almost every other way. They would not look kindly on her taking showers with their son.

"I'm an adult," he said. "They don't get an opinion anymore."

She snorted. "They're still your parents." She hefted the wheelbarrow. "I guarantee they'll have an opinion."

"Whatever." He turned through the gate to the truck, and she turned too, made her way to the shed. She pretended to be straightening the tools, banging them around a little for effect, waiting for him to bring the last load of stone and go for his shower.

She heard the tailgate of the truck slam. When the door of the house opened a moment later, she locked the shed behind her, made her way inside and up the stairs to her bedroom.

The dresser mirror showed her streaked with sweat and soil. Her tanktop, stained even when she had put it on that morning, was filthy, as were the thighs of her shorts where she habitually wiped her hands. She pulled her clothes off and chucked them in the hamper, looked at herself naked in the mirror, something she seldom bothered to do. The grime on her arms and lower legs made her look ridiculous, but she wasn't much to look at anyway, at least not in her own opinion. Her breasts were too small for her satisfaction, or too thin was maybe a better word. They just didn't look as full as other women's. Maybe other women had better bras, she thought. She cupped her breasts in her hands, tried to press them into fullness, but they refused to be shaped as she wanted.

She heard the shower come on next door, and she had a sudden image of Leo's slender, wiry body standing in her tub. She felt a rush of arousal, though she had never thought seriously about him like that before. He was cute, with fine hair that looped in blond curls and an almost delicate face, but he had always been too young to warrant her attention, at least until now apparently, until he had propositioned her in the garden.

This is what you get, she reflected, for hiring a coworker's son. She should have contracted the whole thing out to some fat guy in a too-tight t-shirt, saved herself watching a boy half her age get a tan and grow muscles in her back yard. Saved him watching her in return.

She realized that she had begun to stroke herself, and

she pulled her hand away, embarrassed that she should be feeling this way about him, but she could hardly help herself, not with him naked and youthful and showering just through her bedroom wall. She sat herself on the edge of the bed, spread her thighs a little and began rubbing just beneath the pubic bone, the place she had first learned to pleasure herself. She watched in the mirror as her labia opened to her touch, begging to have her attentions move lower.

She spit in her hand, then slid it to her vagina, splitting her fingers slightly where her clitoris lay hidden, then kneaded the delicate flesh in slow circles. She imagined Leo in the shower, imagined him washing the dirt from his body, his hands trailing to his cock. She slipped a finger into her vagina, quickly added a second. She could get herself off pretty quickly now, she knew, but she also knew it wasn't what she wanted.

"Shit," she said aloud, standing and going for the door all in one motion. She covered the few feet between her room and the bathroom, then paused. Her mind was arguing persuasively that getting into the shower with a boy so young was a stupid idea, but her pussy seemed immune to argument.

She turned the doorknob as quietly as she could. It was unlocked, opening without a sound, and she slipped through the door into the humid heat of the small bathroom. She couldn't see Leo through the shower curtain, but she could hear that he was masturbating, his hand making slick sounds on his cock, his breath coming in pants. The sound filled her with a fear that he would come without her, and she flung aside the curtain as she stepped into the tub.

Leo spun around and slipped back against the wall, almost falling into the tub. "Holy shit!" he yelled, his one hand pressed against the tile, the other still somehow holding his cock.

"Turn around," she said, but he was still too shocked too move. "I said, turn around," she told him again, and this time he seemed to understand, pulling himself to his feet and turning to face the wall.

Wendy stepped up against him, pressed her body to his, reached around to take his cock in her hand. It was soapy, and her hand slid easily. He had softened a little, probably from fright, but he was soon hard again as she played with him, circling his shaft with her fingers, fucking it with firm strokes.

She spread her legs around one of his thighs and began grinding her pussy as she stroked him, undulating herself so that first her breasts and then her groin was pressed against his thin body. The feel of him was delicious, wet and firm. She sped up the motion of her hand and her hips, pleasuring herself as she pleasured him, though it still wasn't what she wanted.

"Slow down," he said at last, "you're making me come," but she ignored him, pressing her hand more firmly into his groin on the downstroke until she felt his cock spasm, watched semen spray onto the floor of the bathtub. He slumped back into her, his breath ragged.

"Now sit," she said, and he did, instantly, as if programmed. His face was level with her hips, the water spraying off her body and settling around him in a mist. She raised one foot and set it on the edge of the tub, spreading her thighs, then she pulled his face into her.

He licked at her feverishly, far more enthusiastic than skillful, his tongue wandering everywhere but staying nowhere long enough to do more than tease. She needed better. She turned around, put the other foot on the edge of the tub, bent forward to give him better access, letting the shower rain down on her back, and he did do better now, finding a rhythm that penetrated her and then drifted down to her clitoris. She still wouldn't come like that, but it would feel good trying. She began grinding herself back against his tongue a little, just enough to heighten the effect. She could feel her sex flush with pleasure.

Suddenly Leo pulled back from her. "I'm hard again," he said, his voice tight. "I need to fuck you."

Wendy wasn't quite ready to stop yet, but she took pity on the need in his voice. She led him from the shower, still dripping, down the few feet of hallway to her bedroom. She pushed him down on the bed, sideways to the mirror. When she looked she could see that her arms and face were still streaked with dirt as she straddled him, took his cock in her hand, and buried it in herself.

She rocked her hips, sliding herself along the length of him, her fingers alternately stroking their two sexes. She slipped one finger into herself along with his cock, right where she knew it would feel best, fucked herself in time to his hips.

"Come soon," she said. "I'm not waiting much longer."

He made a soft groaning sound and started thrusting faster, more sharply. He was looking up at her, his mouth open and panting. "Fuck," he said, a wonderment, and she could feel him spasm against her fingers.

She leaned forward onto him a little, holding his cock in her deeply, rocking in the place where her fingers lay, and then she was coming too.

She leaned back again, hers shoulders slumping. Leo was still looking up at her, and she felt a kind of regret already, a realization that there would be payment for these few minutes of pleasure.

"I wanted that for so long," he said, sliding his hands up her body to cup her breasts. "So long."

She couldn't meet his eyes any longer, looked into the mirror. "Just don't go thinking this is the start of something," she told him, but she saw the reflection of their bodies in the mirror, and she liked the way her breasts looked in his hands.

Just Wear The jeans

"Lily," Alicia said, almost before the door was open, "I can't wear this." She was pulling at the sleeves of her navy skirt suit. It was too large for her in the shoulders, too short in the arms. Its hem fell at an awkward length for her, cutting across her calves in a way that made her seem shapeless.

"Mom, please," Lily replied, looking back by way of the mirror where the hairdresser hovered. "We've had this conversation a thousand times. I don't care what you wear. I didn't care when you bought that outfit, which I agree is awful. And I didn't care when you bought the one before it, which was much better but too slutty. And I didn't care about the one before that, which I can't even remember anymore." She paused as the hairdresser released a clip and began working on another section of hair. "You can wear your pyjamas for all I care. Just show up to the ceremony."

Susan saw the other two bridesmaids smirk at each other.

"I'm just not good at these things," Alicia said. She shrugged uncomfortably in her jacket.

Lily sighed and closed her eyes. "Susan," she said, "can you go help my Mom? You won't need the hairdresser anyway." She looked over to where Susan was half-sitting on the bed, her pixie hair already as it would be when the ceremony rolled around.

Susan could see the pleading in Lily's eyes, the promise that the favour would be made up somehow. "Sure," she said.

She followed Alicia out the bedroom door and up the short set of side-split stairs that led to the master bedroom. Alicia's wide hips seemed to drag Susan along in their wake. She resisted the urge to reach for them, to cup the round buttocks with her hands.

Alicia kicked her low heels across her mostly empty bedroom. They settled beside the bed, incongruous in the otherwise tidy space. She looked at herself in the mirror, half-turning in either direction. "I wouldn't mind dressing my age," she said, "if my age wasn't so damned dowdy."

Susan said nothing, unsure what was wanted of her.

Alicia sighed. "Even the word dowdy is dowdy." She unbuttoned the jacket and threw it behind her on the bed. "Maybe I can wear it without the jacket." She turned back to the mirror and must have seen what Susan saw – a blouse with lace better suited for someone twice her age and the shapeless skirt now looking more awkward than ever. "Damn it," she said. "Why can't you just wear jeans to these things?"

The question was one that Susan had asked herself often enough recently. This was her third bridal party of the summer, though the dresses this time were at least simple enough to wear again. Even so, jeans sounded good.

She looked up to see Alicia trying to undo the mother-of-pearl buttons that ran down the back of the too-lacy blouse. "Let me help," she said, and she stepped behind the mother of the bride, began unfastening the thirty or so buttons. "How did you ever do these up?"

"Lily helped."

"I see." Alicia wasn't wearing any perfume, but her hair smelled good. She leaned down against the dresser as Susan worked down her back, pulling her hair ever further away but pushing out her buttocks to brush against Susan's groin.

The touch filled Susan with need. She pretended to fumble with a particularly difficult button, leaned in a little to press herself against Alicia's ass, only barely kept herself from grinding herself openly against the older woman's roundness. "There," she said, "done," and she stepped back, though her pussy wanted more.

She watched Alicia pull the blouse over her head to reveal full, freckled breasts in a bra almost as lacy as the shirt that had covered it, though this lace didn't suit her any better. She really was a jeans woman.

Alicia unzipped her skirt and let it fall to the floor, then she cocked her hips in the mirror. She looked much better in just her panties, even if they were the match of her bra, too fancy for the woman who wore them. At least they showed her round thighs, her still trim waist, her shapely calves. She seemed to be considering her reflection.

Susan looked at the other woman's body, imagined running her hands over those hips and thighs. "Do you have something else to try?" she asked, though what she really wanted was to slip the panties off and find Alicia's pussy with her tongue.

"Not really. The first dress I bought is too big now that I lost that weight, and the second one shows a bit too much for a wedding. I can't believe the girl convinced me to get it."

"Well, how about we try the second one? Maybe we can make it work."

Alicia shrugged and went to the closet, her wide dimpled ass swinging as she walked. She pulled a black dress from the closet and held it in front of her as she turned. "What do you think?" she asked.

"It's hard to say before it's on."

She slipped it from the hanger and stepped into it, pulling it up to her waist. The material clung to her, showing her shape better but also bunching in places. She reached behind and unclasped her bra. "The problem is that I can't wear a bra with this one," she said, her breasts swinging heavily as she bent to pull the straps of the dress onto her arms.

Susan wanted to stop her, to go and hold her freckled breasts, but Alicia soon covered them again, though the neckline was deep enough to expose more than the bra had.

"I could've done it at twenty," Alicia said, returning to the mirror, trying to arrange the dress to her satisfaction. "Maybe even thirty," she added after a moment, and Susan wanted to comfort her, to tell her that her breasts looked better bare anyway.

"We could go buy those stick-on supports," she offered, but Alicia shook her head.

"No. I'll just wear the dowdy thing." She made a face. "It's not like anyone will be taking pictures at a wedding." She slipped the straps of the dress from her arms, and her breasts swung free again, their broad nipples swaying, needing to be held.

Susan was a few feet away, but crossed them in single step and wrapped her arms around the Alicia from behind, gathering her breasts in her hands. "Maybe you should just wear jeans," she said, calmly, as if she hadn't pressed herself against another woman's half naked body.

Alicia tried to turn, but Susan held her, pressing her face into Alicia's neck and kissing up to her ear. She felt the other woman's nipples harden in her hands, looked in the mirror to see them pucker between her fingers.

Alicia's body was as rigid as her nipples. "I. . . I've. . . " she said.

"Please," Susan said, "please let me show you." She

dropped one hand to the dress that still clung to Alicia's hips, pulling it down until it fell free to the floor. Alicia didn't even step out of the fallen fabric as Susan held herself against the older woman's body, still cupping a breast with one hand, trailing the other against the lace between her legs.

"The wedding is in..." said Alicia.

"Three hours," replied Susan.

Alicia seemed to consider this, and then something in her relented. She let her head roll back so that Susan could kiss her throat, and she reached down herself to slip off her panties, standing with her legs slightly spread.

Susan cupped Alicia's sex and began stroking gently, combing her fingers through the pubic hair and pressing lightly where the clitoris was concealed. Her own pussy was aching, full of need. "Lay down on the bed," she said.

There was no hesitation in Alicia now. She moved to the bed, swaying her full ass, and she laid on her back, pulling her legs up to expose her pussy. "Like this?"

Susan was too full of lust to answer. She undid the side zipper of her dress, wriggled out of it, then laid her face between Alicia's thighs, her tongue searching out the other woman's pussy, licking, teasing, sucking, too desperate even to do the job right, as if it was her first time.

Alicia's hand dropped to Susan's head and begin playing with her pixie-short hair. Her throat make a little moan of pleasure. "Wow," she said softly, "that feels wonderful."

Susan began licking in earnest now, finding the rhythm that she knew would please most, more deft, less frenzied.

"You're going to make me come," Alicia said, her breath panting.

Susan slid her hands under Alicia's buttocks, filled her hands with their soft roundness, drew them up to meet her mouth, kneading them in time with her tongue. She felt Alicia's body tense, quiver, and then almost collapse into her hands.

"I've never been fucked that good."

"I'm not done," said Susan, because the need in her had only grown, the need for Alicia's body, her full and soft and rounded body. Susan stood just long enough to remove her own bra and panties, then she lay between Alicia's thighs, her face between Alicia's breasts, her sex pressed against Alicia's.

"Show me how," Alicia said, but Susan couldn't answer. She took a freckled breast in her mouth, not the nipple only, but as much breast as she could, filling her mouth with it. She wriggled herself against the wetness of the pussy beneath her, found the place where the pubic bone fit best, pleasured herself, coming to the point of orgasm almost immediately, then keeping herself there, on the cusp, holding the sensation inside her.

"I thought you had a boyfriend," Alicia said, her voice sounding dreamy and sex drunk.

The words took a few moments to find their way through Susan's clenched pleasure. "I do," she said, though even her own words seemed to come from far away.

"Then why..."

"Because I need both," she said, and that seemed trigger enough for her orgasm. She rocked herself on Alicia's body, the release washing through her, hearing the sound of the other woman's breathing, smelling her, tasting her.

Susan laid her head down between Alicia's breasts, felt the rise and fall of her chest. "I'll wear jeans to the ceremony," she said, "if you do."

Trust the Universe

"Well, go fuck him then." Lilith rolled up her pillow and tucked it beneath the side of her head. She lay on her side, her body undulating from shoulder to waist, from hip to feet, naked, as she almost always was in bed, in contrast to Suri's habitual cotton sleep shirt.

Suri scrunched her face, looked past her lover to the door of their room, the lock on the antique glass doorknob safely thrown. "I'm not sure I want to," she said, but she did. There was something in her that was drawn to him, to the way he turned his head so he could better hear what she had to say, the way he put his hand on her shoulder when he said good morning at the breakfast table. Hell, and the way she imagined he would make love to her. She may as well stop denying it.

"Don't fool yourself. You clearly want to fuck him," Lilith said. "Though why you'd want to trade this trim little package. . . " she reached down to cup her sex ". . . for some dangly old dick is entirely beyond me."

"It's not trading. . . " Suri said, but she didn't know how to finish the sentence. The ache she felt for a man sometimes, for this man now, defied her ability to explain.

She wanted to be full of him, and that was all.

"Well, he's certainly got it on offer." Lilith was playing at banter, probably meant most of it, but Suri felt the hurt beneath her tone.

"You keep saying that, but he only ever hints..."

Lilith sniffed. "He let you know that he leaves his door unlocked at night."

Suri reached out and put her hand on Lilith's arm, traced it down to where her fingertips gave way to hip. "Only because I told him it was unlocked when I went to change the linen."

"Yup, and then he looked right at you and said that he never locks it, even when he's sleeping. Said it was important to trust the universe sometimes." She snared Suri's hand in her own.

"Maybe it is important," Suri said, and for a moment she forgot that she was talking about whether to sleep with a man who had stayed in her bed and breakfast too many times, who had somewhere along the line stopped being simply a guest. She saw him, saw Alfred, saying just that – "Sometimes you need to trust the universe." She hadn't known what to say then and didn't now. In her experience, the universe seldom rewarded trust.

"You're drifting," said Lilith, which is what she always said when Suri started thinking too much, started losing contact with the conversation.

"Sorry."

"Don't apologize. Just make up your mind." She drew Suri's hand up between her cheek and her shoulder. "You can either stay here, in which case you need to turn off the light so that we can get some sleep. Or you can go fuck him, in which case you need to change into something a little more alluring than that shapeless shirt."

"You've never complained about my shirt before."

"Because I know what's under it. I recommend something more suggestive for a man who's yet to be enlightened."

Suri rolled from the bed and opened her top drawer. She hadn't needed it much recently. Lilith was unimpressed by lingerie, preferred nudity, merely put up with everything else. Suri hadn't worn anything from that drawer since her last boy, months ago now, maybe more than a year, long enough for the need in her to get pretty damn strong.

"So, that means you're going?"

Suri shrugged, pulled her t-shirt over her head and tossed it onto her pillow.

"You should go just like that," Lilith said. She gave an exaggerated wink. "Or you could stay here just like that."

Suri pulled out a cream nightie, lace at the top flowing into a close fitting skirt. She pulled it over her head, settled it around herself, plumped her breasts up in the mirror, admired the contrast between the cream silk and her dark skin. She imagined what Alfred would think when she came into his room, then shook her head. The whole thing was ridiculous. What if he just threw her out?

"You looked better naked," said Lilith, "but that outfit should get you some cock."

Which was what Suri wanted, truthfully, however much she wished she could be content to lie back down in her own bed, pull Lilith's thigh up over her body, nestle into the other woman's softness. But she wanted cock, and she had no way to explain why, not even to herself, never mind Lilith.

She turned back to the bed. "I'm sorry," she said. "I don't know why I need this."

Lilith gave a shrugging smile. "Well, don't ask me," she said. "I don't know why you'd want some nasty man."

Suri sighed, looked back to the mirror, but Lilith rolled herself suddenly out of bed and gathered Suri to her, sliding her hands up beneath the nightie. "It's okay," she said, her voice as serious as Suri had ever heard it. "Really." And then she was smiling again. "I knew you were a strange one before I ever dragged you into my bed." She kissed Suri, a gentle pulling kind of kiss.

"Are you sure?"

"Sure as I'm gonna be." She slapped Suri's bottom with both hands and gave her a nudge toward the door.

"Now go show him what my girl can do. You hear me?" She wagged her finger with mock severity.

Suri exchanged a smile with her, unlocked the door and slipped into the hall. The emergency light made sharp shadows in the back stairwell down to the guest rooms, and the stairs creaked occasionally, an eerie sound. She wondered whether she'd be in any mood to seduce Alfred by the time she got to his room, but it was a needless worry. The longing in her was undiminished as she stopped outside his room. She listened for signs of wakefulness, but there were none. The whole house was silent. She turned the glass handle of the door, the match to her own. It was unlocked as he said it would be, swinging without a sound on the hinges she herself oiled each fall.

It was a small room. Most of them were. She could touch the foot of the bed as she closed the door behind her and turned the lock. The shape of Alfred's body was stretched beneath the quilt, lying on his back. One of his arms was thrown over his head against the wall, the other lay on his stomach atop the covers. She looked at him, listened to his heavy breath, watched the quilt rise and fall with his chest, wondered what to do now that she had come this far. Should she crawl into bed beside him, wake him gently with kisses, or should she just tear off the blankets, pull down his pants, put her mouth on his cock?

She reached for the covers, drew them a little aside, and then decided suddenly to straddle him, cover him

69

with her body. His hands started as she settled her weight on him. He tried instinctively to push her away, but his attempts were clumsy with sleep. He looked as confused by his surroundings as by the woman atop him. "Where..." he began, but she bent down and kissed him, felt the previous day's beard scuff her lips and face.

He pushed her back a little, tried to make eye contact, but she buried her face in his shoulder. "Take your pants off," she said into his ear.

He hesitated a moment, but she dragged her hips up his body, pressed her breasts into his face, and then he was undoing the drawstring of his pajamas, pushing them off first with his hands and then with his feet. He was already hardening between her thighs.

She slid down again, felt the shaft of his cock against her sex. "Touch me," she told him, and he did, sliding his hands up the back of her thighs, parting her buttocks beneath the skirt that had already ridden up around her waist. "My pussy," she said. "Touch my pussy."

He pulled one of her thighs up along his body, searched out her wetness with his other hand, and she was truly wet now, slick on his fingers. It never took her long, and she didn't feel much like waiting tonight, just wanted to fill the need in her and get back to Lilith's bed.

She sat up astride him, took his cock in her hand, lowered herself onto it. She felt the fullness of it and let herself groan out loud.

He ran his hands up her body, pulled the top of her

nightie down, spilled her breasts out. She let him draw her back down against him, his mouth finding her nipples, suckling her as she circled her hips on him.

"Put your fingers in me," she said. "With your cock. Fill me up."

He obeyed, and it was good, but it wasn't enough, and she started to feel frantic that the ache in her would go on aching even now after she had got what she thought she needed. "Put your finger in my ass," she said. Her voice was thick with desperation, almost a growl.

"What?"

She put her mouth by his ear. "Do it," she said, as hard and clear and she could manage in a whisper. "Put your finger in my ass."

His finger, slick with her wetness, pressed against her anus, penetrated her a little, and she leaned into it slowly, felt the double fullness of his cock and his finger.

"Again," she said. "Get it wet, and put it in me again."

He did as he was told, his hips almost motionless now, his fingers moving from the dampness of her pussy to the tightness of her ass.

"Now deeper," she said, and she leaned back onto him.

"I'm gonna come," he warned, his free hand clutching at her side below her breast.

She forced herself to pull off of him. "Don't you dare," she said. She wouldn't be able to wait for him to get it up a second time, wouldn't be able to face the quiet of his bed that long.

His eyes were closed beneath her. "I'm okay now," he said at last.

"Don't move," she told him, and then she raised herself over his cock again. She ran her fingers across her pussy to her ass, lubricating it still more, then she placed him against her anus, lowered herself slowly onto him. The pressure was both a pain and a pleasure, a filling up that went past fullness, and then she felt him in her. She bobbed there a moment, just slightly, reveling in it, her fingers making circles of her sex, slick circles of pleasure.

He thrust into her a little further, too far, too quickly. "No!" she said. "Don't move," and he lay quiet beneath her again.

She pressed herself down on him as slowly as she could, drawing out the sensation, not so much fucking his cock as enveloping it, taking possession of it, all of it, deeply, and then she rocked on him, stroking herself with her fingers, letting the pleasure build until it rolled over her. She leaned forward involuntarily, her orgasm rounding her shoulders.

"Okay," she said. "You can come now," and it took him only a couple of thrusts before she felt him spasm in the tightness of her ass.

She let him wallow for a moment, softening, and then drew herself off him, gingerly, felt the emptiness like an absence. Her nightie slipped down around her hips again

72

as she knelt and drew its straps up over her shoulders. "Good night," she said, meeting his eyes for the barest moment.

"Good night," he echoed. He looked like he wanted to say more, but she left him before he could try.

She made her way to her own room almost without noticing, found herself slipping through the door, wondering whether Lilith was still awake, what she would say if she was.

The covers had been laid open, waiting for her, and she nestled into her pillow before drawing them over her, not yet brave enough to reach for her lover, not with the feeling of Albert's cock still lingering in her, but Lilith reached for her as soon as she laid down, drew her close.

"You stink like man," Lilith said.

"Sorry."

"Yeah, well. It's to be expected." She paused. "How'd it go?"

Suri smiled against Lilith's bare shoulder. "Let's just say it might be awkward serving breakfast in the morning."

"Really? How crazy could it get in fifteen minutes?"

"Well. . ." Suri burrowed down to press her face between Lilith's breasts. "I may have fucked him in my ass."

Lilith laughed quietly, her breasts shaking against Suri's face. "You're right. I should take care of breakfast," she said.

"That might be a good idea." There was quiet for a long moment, and Suri realized that the ache in her had gone, though she couldn't remember exactly when it left, whether in Alfred's bed or in Lilith's. "Shit," she said, because the thought had triggered her memory somehow, "I forgot to lock our door."

She tried to roll out of bed, but Lilith held her, ran a hand through her hair, kissed her forehead. "Don't worry about it," she said. "Sometimes you just need to trust the universe."

Now Is Best

The knock only half-woke Thomas, just enough for him to wonder who could be at his door at almost an hour after midnight. He was already out of bed and across the unfamiliar room before he remembered that he was in the college's guest cottage. He was still processing this idea when he opened the door and found a girl standing there, one of the students from the reading that afternoon.

"Hello?" he asked, flicking on the light. "What can I do for you?"

"You said you'd look at my poems." She passed by him into the cottage, setting a notebook down on the table, carrying herself with a confidence so complete it looked like boredom.

He did actually remember saying something of that sort to her, as he had said to perhaps a dozen earnest young writers that afternoon. "Yes, of course, I'd be glad to look at them," he said, "but it's really late. Maybe you could email them to me, or we could arrange a time to meet in the library before I leave."

"Now would be best," she said, picking at the gift basket of fruit and cheese and crackers that the college had presented him after his reading. "You can't really say anything over email, and we'd be interrupted a hundred times in the library." She began to peel an orange. "Now is best."

He picked up the notebook and leaned back against the table, half-sitting on it, still too groggy really to decide firmly about anything. The first poem was much better than he expected, much better than the stuff he normally saw from college students. The name in the corner read Bristol Lawler, and he remembered the name from earlier on, one of a hundred or so, but unique enough to remain with him.

"How long have you been writing?" he asked.

"As long as I can remember." She had made a neat pile of the orange peels, sectioned each slice meticulously. She popped one section into her mouth, chewed, swallowed. "I still have poems from when I was six or seven." She ate another slice. "They're not good."

"Well," he said, "this first one here is pretty good. It's very tightly structured, develops the central image beautifully, has a good sense of rhythm." She nodded as if all that was perfectly obvious. "I think the line endings need a little work, and there are some dead words here that need to be replaced, but overall..."

"Line endings?" she asked, leaning in to see over his arm, her hand on the table behind him.

"Yeah." He pointed at the second stanza. "See how this line ends in 'worlds'? Well, think how much stronger

76

it would be if you rewrote it to end in 'skin', which is the word that speaks most to the central image."

"I see," she said, and she reached across him to trace the line he was describing with her finger. Her breast pressed against his arm, firm and youthful breast. His penis responded, and he suddenly realized how vulnerable a position he was in, a fact that he had overlooked first because of grogginess and then because of surprise at her poetry.

"It really is late," he said, trying to sound nonchalant. "You should probably go."

She turned the page of the notebook, her breast still pressing his arm. "Just a few more," she said.

He was fully erect now, trying to think of how he might extricate himself from the situation without revealing his condition. He stalled by reading a little of the next poem, hoping his body would have time to calm itself. The second poem seemed to stumble in its cadence almost immediately. "This second line doesn't read smoothly," he said.

"Let me hear how you're reading it," she said, and he was about to begin when he felt her hand on his penis.

"What the hell do you think you're doing?" he asked. He had instinctively jerked away and was now looking at her over the corner of the table."

"I was stroking your cock," she said. Her expression still showed only bored self-assurance, her hip leaning against the table as if it had leaned there a thousand times before, confident in the beauty that her youthful prettiness promised to become.

"Well, it's completely inappropriate," he said, sounding awkward even to himself. "You need to leave."

"Listen, Mr. Kenalty," she said, with the disinterested calm of a class speech, "we're both adults. And there's no conflict of interest here. You aren't a teacher. You have no influence on my marks or anything else. The only rule being broken is my curfew." She pointed to her notebook, still in his hand. "I've gone to a lot of trouble to sneak out of dorm tonight, so I want you to read those for me, and I want you to give me feedback on them, and I want you to stop freaking out about a woman putting her hand on your cock." She said all this quietly and evenly, without the slightest sign of anger, but there was something in her voice that did not permit refusal.

She rounded the corner of the table, lifted his hand with the notebook to where he could read it, then slid her hand down the front of his pyjama pants to grab his naked cock. "Read," she said, and she started to stroke him with evident practise.

He began to read the poem in front of him almost against his will. The second line was the awkward one, and she interrupted him when he finished it. "Yes," she said, "You're right. I was hearing it differently, but you're right." She kept touching him all the time, never bringing him anywhere close to orgasm, just teasing him. "Keep going," she said.

The poem ran only twenty lines or so, but she stopped him twice more, asking about certain lines, certain words, but always with the same flat competence. She was good, he realized, not only by instinct but also by practice, still raw in many ways, but knowledgeable in her craft.

When he had finished reading, she read it aloud in turn, correcting several lines as she did.

"That's much better," he said, because it was.

"Read the next one," she told him, and she dropped to her knees as he turned the page, pulled his pants down around his hips, took his cock in her mouth. He flinched instinctively but didn't pull away. There was something in her certainty that he could not defy.

He began the third poem, but he struggled to focus through the feeling of her tongue, not exactly sucking him, only teasing, as she had with her fingers, searching out his most sensitive pleasures. "Focus," she said, kissing the tip of his penis, "I need to hear the rhythm of it."

He began again, forcing himself to ignore her, even as she took the length of his cock in her hand and began stroking it firmly, an extension of her mouth and tongue. He felt need build in him, coming somehow as much from the words he was reading as from the feeling of her mouth on his cock. The poem built in him like an orgasm, but she wouldn't let him finish when it did.

She took him from her mouth but kept stroking him. "Well," she said, "any suggestions on that one?"

79

He couldn't remember much of the poem, certainly not with the clarity needed to critique it. "No," he said. "I think it works pretty well."

She stood and pulled her sweater over her head. "I'll read one now," she said, but she didn't take the book from him. Instead she reached behind her to unclasp her bra and free her breasts, small and youthful and impertinent. She stepped close to him so that they were pressed against his chest, and he could feel her nipples through his shirt. She undid his shirt from the bottom up, but didn't remove it, just opened it far enough for her chest to touch his, undulating her body so that her breasts drew arcane symbols on his body.

She stepped back from him after a moment, but still made no attempt to take the notebook. Instead she slid her pants down her legs, left them in a pile, then took her panties off too, set them on top. She stood there, her hips cocked, round and firm. "Give me the book," she said, and he reached out for her to take it.

It was still open to the third poem. She turned the page, then hopped up to sit on the table, wiggling herself backward until her legs were halfway on the table too, the first girlish act he had seen in her. She leaned back on one hand, held the book up with the other, then drew her knees up, spreading her thighs. "Lick me while I read," she said, and there was no refusing her.

He couldn't reach her from his knees, so he had to crouch and lean awkwardly across the table, his hands scooping her full buttocks. He traced her already open labia with his tongue, tentative, but she placed the hand holding the book behind his head and drew him into her. The scent and taste of her filled him, filled not just his mouth, it seemed, but all of him, and her reading filled him too, though he hardly heard it, only felt it, like something that also needed to be tasted. He plunged his tongue into her, needing more of it, but also alarmed at his need, alarmed that a girl he hardly knew should have such control over him.

The poem was finished in a few moments, but he didn't hear it, only felt the book being laid down and her hand returning to his head, idly playing with his hair. She made no sound at all, gave almost no sign of pleasure, as if he were merely painting her toenails or shining her shoes.

"Stand up," she said at last, and she pushed herself off of the table, then turned and bent over it, her legs spread and her ass raised to him. "You can come in me now," she said. "Nice and hard."

There was something about her detachment that he found disconcerting, unattractive even, but he was too full of lust now, even if he could have discovered the secret to defying her. He stepped behind her and placed his cock on her pussy, not entering her yet, just pressing her open a little, letting himself take pleasure from her. He toyed with himself there, slipping into her just enough to keep the sensation.

"I told you nice and hard," she said after a moment, and there was a hint of some emotion in her for the first time, some anger or annoyance.

"Wait," he said, and he pulled himself away from her pussy entirely, letting his cock slide between the cheeks of her ass, enjoying the site of his penis pressed against her. He pleasured himself there, kneading the flesh of her buttocks in his hands, pressing it around his cock. He felt himself approaching orgasm and wondered whether just to let himself come on the roundness of her ass.

"Please," she said, a note of desperation in her voice, a break in her disinterested exterior.

The idea stopped him, cock resting on her bottom. "Do you need it?" he asked, sincerely asking, suddenly free of whatever spell she had been exercising on him.

"Yes," she said, pressing her hips back against him. "I need it." She sounded her age at last, a young woman, newly adult, laying aside a mask of detachment that she could no longer maintain.

He took his cock in his hand and drove into her. She ground herself back onto him, enveloping him, and he fucked her quickly, not worrying about her pleasure, letting his orgasm come when it would.

He slowed his hips, let his cock wallow in the pleasure of her pussy. She laid her head down on the table, her notebook clutched in her hand. "Yes," she said, her voice hardly audible. "I need it."

Back on Your Feet

The phone rang from under a pile of papers on the dining-room table. Gail dug it out blindly, still absorbed in the video editor on her laptop.

"Hello?"

"Gail. It's Lori." She sounded hurried, harassed. "I know it's short notice, but Dale just called and said he can't pick up the kids from school. Can you get them for me?"

Gail looked at the stuff strewn across the table, at least a few more hours of work, and Perry wouldn't be happy if the spot wasn't ready tomorrow. "You can't get away?"

"I asked my manager, but it's too late to call some-one in." There was a creeping bitterness to her voice. "Cashiers in grocery stores don't have much pull."

"Okay. I'll go up and get the kids. 3:15, right?"

"Yeah. Thanks for doing this."

"No problem. You'll come pick them up at..."

"Well, I'm off at 5:00, so I can probably be there by 5:30, assuming the buses are running on time."

"I could come get you."

83

"Ben still needs a booster seat, and you won't have one. I'll just bus it."

Gail looked at the time as she hung up, only an hour before she'd have to walk up to the school. She made herself a calendar reminder to alert her at 3:00, and it seemed only moments, mostly unproductive moments, before it chirped at her.

A swarm of parents already waited outside the school as she approached, neighbours all, but she didn't know any of them very well, didn't even recognize most of them. They were the wrong age, the wrong stage of life, too young and too involved with their young families to bother with a couple like Gail and Ryan, childless at almost fifty.

Lori would have fit better – younger and hipper and the mother of two small kids. Gail imagined Lori mingling with the other parents, confident in her trendy clothes and her trim figure and her beautiful children. Gail would have given a lot to have all three of those things, though not if she got Lori's ex-husband in the bargain.

Dale was a profound example of why not to go home with a guy just because he was cute, why not to marry him even once you found out he was fucking around on you, and why not to have babies with him even after he also turned out to be a deadbeat. She wondered what had kept him from picking up his kids today, suspected it had to do with drinking or gambling or both.

84

She had tried to warn Lori about him from the beginning, when Lori was still a student and renting their basement apartment, but Dale was cute, and he was charming, and he was apparently also quite good in bed, and nothing Gail could say had been convincing. She wished now that she had been firmer about it, but she couldn't have predicted quite how bad things would be, and at the time she had also been distracted by things like how nice it would be to have Lori in her own bed, with her long athlete's legs and the smooth curve of her neck.

The children interrupted her recollections, appearing in a rush from the side door of the school. She called them over, explained why they were coming to her house, steered them toward home. Snack food didn't figure prominently on her regular grocery list, so she stopped at the corner store for a big bag of caramel popcorn, then seated the kids and the popcorn bowl in front of the television. "You guys find something to watch," she said, which was probably bad parenting, but then, she wasn't their parent.

She transferred a casserole from the freezer to the oven and returned to her work. It went better now, and she was almost finished by the time Lori came knocking at the door.

"Thanks so much for doing this," Lori said. She was as pretty as Gail remembered, but thinner now, too thin, her eyes tired, a grimness to the way she pressed her lips together.

Gail felt a sudden pity for her, though it was a pity mixed with desire, an urge to take the girl in, care for her, make love to her. "Why don't you stay for supper?" she said.

"No, I'm sure you have stuff to do."

"It's no trouble. I've got a big casserole in the oven, and Ryan will be home any minute. We'll have supper together before you guys head home."

"I have to take the kids to Dale's place at 7:00, so we'd have to leave pretty soon to get the buses anyway."

"Well, let us drive you then. It won't hurt Ben to go without a booster seat just this once."

The younger woman seemed about to resist further, but Gail took her by the elbow, letting her fingers linger as she drew her into the house, helped her off with her jacket. Lori seemed to surrender.

She insisted on setting the table for Gail, made sure her kids finished everything put in front of them, and ate two large helpings herself, clearly forcing herself not to eat too fast.

Gail sat close to her, leaning toward her as they spoke, taking every opportunity to touch her on the shoulder, the hand, the elbow. "Is there anything you need a car for?" she asked. "I have some time tonight. We could do a grocery run or something. Whatever you need."

Lori opened her mouth to say something, but stopped. She had always seemed so beautiful to Gail, so perfectly a woman, but now the beauty was haunted, her old strength ebbed away through months of divorce courts, single-parenting, stop-gap jobs, and too little income.

"I know money's tight for you right now." Gail put her hand on Lori's thigh. She tried to tell herself that it was a gesture of comfort, but she knew how mixed it was with lust. "We'll cover the groceries tonight."

"Absolutely," Ryan said. "Our way of helping you get back on your feet."

Lori ducked her head, letting her hair fall across her face. "That would be great," she said. "I..." She took the hand that Gail had laid on her thigh and squeezed it.

"Don't worry about it," said Gail. "Now, let's pack those kids up and get moving."

Ryan stood and began clearing the table, giving Gail his best leer as he passed. She pinched his ass with the hand that wasn't in Lori's lap. "The house had better be spic and span when I get back," she told him, "or there'll be hell to pay."

"I live only to serve, great mistress," he replied.

It took a while to herd the kids into the car, so it was actually a few minutes past 7:00 when they finally arrived at Dale's place, the apartment his parents were letting him use in their basement.

"He'll be pissed at me," Lori said, though too low for the kids to hear from the backseat.

"For what? For having to pick up the kids on his night?"

"For being late."

"Ten minutes maybe."

Lori shrugged. "Enough to give him an excuse."

"I'll take them up," Gail said. "You just wait here."

"It's okay, I'll..." Lori began, but Gail was already out of the car and collecting the kids, leading them up the driveway to the sidedoor.

"What the fuck?" Dale said, almost before the door was open. "Where's Lori? She was supposed to have the kids here like ten minutes ago." His face was unshaven. The smell of sweat and alcohol hung faint but clear on his rumpled clothes.

"Oh, I'm just helping her out with the kids tonight because somebody didn't get around to picking them up from school today."

"Don't get smart-assed with me, Gail. I was at a job interview."

"Really? A job interview that just came up without warning at 2:30 in the afternoon? Exactly what kind of job were you applying for?"

"None of your business."

"Well, I'm glad to see that you cleaned up for it at least. I'm sure the week-old scruff made a really great impression."

"Fuck you, Gail."

"Have a good night, Dale." She turned back down the driveway to the car.

"Bitch!" he yelled after her, but she ignored him, slid in behind the wheel.

"How'd it go?" Lori asked, her eyes wary.

"Oh, we had a great little chat."

Lori looked dubious.

Gail put her hand on Lori's leg again, for the second time that evening, stroked the too-thin flesh comfortingly, felt a rush of desire between her thighs. "It went fine. Now relax. Let's go shopping."

Lori said nothing on the way to the store, said very little even as they were shopping, mostly filling the cart in silence. Gail added things as well, things she knew the kids would like – chocolate covered granola bars – or that Lori would appreciate but was too considerate to take when someone else would be paying the bill – fresh-made sushi and some good quality icecream. Gail also bought two bottles of wine at the kiosk on the way out, not very good wine, but the best they had, drinkable. Lori tried to refuse, but Gail would have none of her objections.

There were quite a few groceries, and Lori's little apartment was in the attic of an older home, so Gail followed Lori's lithe legs up the exterior stairs a half dozen times before they were done, desire growing all the time, wanting nothing more than to take the slender body in her hands.

"Where are the wine glasses?" she asked when they were finished, pulling the bottles from the paper bag.

"I don't have any, but the corkscrew is in the cutlery drawer there."

Gail pulled the cork, took two of the larger tumblers from the drying rack beside the sink, poured them as full as she dared, a good third of the bottle into each. She took a swallow from her own. Lori was kneeling in front of the fridge, putting vegetables in the crisper, so Gail sat behind her, leaning back against the cupboard.

"Here's yours," she said, holding out the other glass. Lori took it, sipped from it delicately, put it on the counter above her. Gail watched her putting things away until the bags were empty and the fridge was closed, then she patted the floor between her spread legs. "I've got a spot for you right here."

Lori looked at her for a moment, as if deciding what all was implied in the invitation, then sat herself between Gail's legs, leaned back into the older woman's chest, held her cup of wine on her belly.

Gail brushed Lori's hair back out of her face, drew the back of her hand along Lori's cheek, jaw, neck, collarbone, right to the top button of her blouse, then back again, stroking gently.

Lori turned her head a little, opening herself to Gail's hand, nestling herself against the older woman's breasts. She lowered one hand from her cup and rested it along Gail's thigh, pulling it closer against her.

There was a long silence. Lori finished her wine and set the cup aside.

90

Gail let her fingers trail to the top button of Lori's blouse, pulled it open, then the next, slipped her hand inside Lori's bra to cup her small breast. The younger woman's ribs felt thin and fragile beneath her touch.

"I should probably get some housework done," Lori said, "but I really just want to lay here and let you touch me."

Gail caressed the top of her breast, teased her nipple between her fingertips. "Then just lay here and let me touch you." She laid her other hand on Lori's belly, untucked her shirt, unbuttoned her pants. Her fingers slid over Lori's panties to cup her sex, framed by wisps of hair, hot in her hand.

Lori exhaled long and soft, a sound more suited to meditation than arousal. She pressed her hips forward against Gail's touch, used her own hands to grip Gail's thighs.

The ache in Gail's own sex was almost unbearable. She pressed herself a little against Lori's back as she stroked the other woman through her panties, pretending it was her own pussy beneath her fingers.

"Please," said Lori, undulating herself gently, only just enough to be felt, first back against Gail's body and then forward against her fingers. "Please touch me."

Gail took Lori's panties by the crotch, pulled them to the side. She found the younger woman's wetness, circled it, then slipped a finger into her.

The sigh that Lori gave was no longer meditative.

She pressed herself against Gail's fingers, slowly at first, but ever faster, until she was almost quivering with little gyrations. "Harder," she said, and then she put her own hand down her pants as well, covered Gail's hand with her own, pressing hard against her pubic bone.

Gail put a second finger into Lori's vagina, slick now with wetness, plump with desire.

"Yes," Lori said. "More."

Gail added a third finger, and Lori made a noise almost like a growl, lifting her hips from the floor and stroking wildly with their two hands, using Gail's fingers almost against her will.

"Fuck," she said, her body clenching, and then she seemed almost to collapse, her head falling back again onto Gail's breasts, her body finding the safety of the older woman's embrace. She shuddered.

"Thanks," she said, and then a moment later, "for picking up the kids."

About the Author

Robin Elizabeth Downey was born in Toronto, Ontario in 1952. She was bisexual long before most people knew exactly what that was. She never married but has two adult children. She writes erotica because it's the last literary genre that has something left to say. She also writes poetry, whether or not it has something left to say. She now makes her home in Guelph, Ontario.